Space Dog

to the Rescue

Vivian French
Illustrated by Sue Heap

Hodder Children's Books

a division of Hodder Headline plc

For Tom

this book belongs to

. . . .

A Catalogue record for this book is available from the British
Library

ISBN 0340 71363 1

Printed and bound in Great Britain by
The Devonshire Press, Torquay, Devon TQ2 7NX

Hodder Children's Books
A Division of Hodder Headline plc
338 Euston Road
London NW1 3BH

CHAPTER ONE

It was very early in the morning.

Blue Moon was just off to bed.

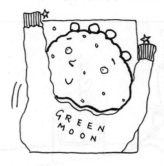

Green Moon was putting on her pyjamas.

Purple Moon was fast asleep.

Big Sun was getting ready to shine.

Little Sun was yawning . . .

and inside the Space Kennel Space Dog was stretching.

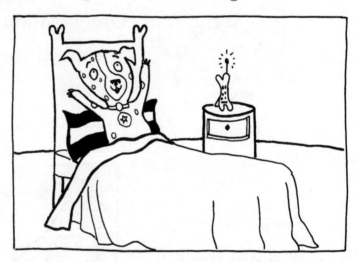

"WOOF!" he said. "Is it time to get up yet?"

BRRRRRINGGGGGGGG!!!!!!!

It was the
bone phone.

Space Dog answered it.
"Hi! Space Dog here! How can
I help you?"

3

"BEEEEP!" said a voice.
"BEEEEP!" and then there
was silence.

"WOOF! WOOF!" Space Dog
leapt up. "It's Planet Beep! The
Beepers must be in trouble!
Away I go!"

And off Space Dog flew . . .
past Blue Moon, past Green
Moon, past Purple Moon.

Blue Moon
stopped
and stared.

Green Moon
waved her
toothbrush.

Purple Moon
stayed fast
asleep.

On and on flew Space Dog.
At last he saw Beeper Moon
ahead, just above Planet Beep.

"She's up late," Space Dog
thought as he zoomed past.
"Very late . . .

WOOOOOOOOOOOOOFFF!!!"
Space Dog stopped.

Something was very wrong!
Beeper Moon was dripping.
Drip . . . drip . . . drip.

"You're MELTING!" said Space
Dog.
Beeper Moon sighed.
"I'm NOT melting," she said.
"I'm CRYING!"

"Oh," said Space Dog. "WHY
are you crying, Beeper Moon?"

Beeper Moon gave another
huge sigh.

"Because I'm lonely.
I shine away all night long.
Does anyone ever talk to me?
NO."

Does anybody EVER tell me a joke? NO!

I love jokes.

She dripped
faster than ever.

"Woof!" said
Space Dog.
"PLEASE don't
cry. Let me
see what I can do."

"Not much,"
said Beeper
Moon. She
wiped her nose
in a squishy
squashy way.
"Maybe I'll go
to bed."

"You are up very late,"
Space Dog said.
"Big Sun's been up for ages!"

Beeper Moon wailed.

"I stay up late so that the Beepers will see me and say 'Thank you, Beeper Moon'."

Or even, 'Let me tell you a joke, Beeper Moon!' But do they?

NOOOOOOOOOO!!

And she shook
all over.

"There, there." Space Dog patted Beeper Moon's fat cheesy green face.

"Be a good moon and blow your nose. Tuck yourself into bed. I'll be back soon."

Beeper Moon sniffled herself into her bed of clouds.
And Space Dog flew on down to Planet Beep.

"WOOF!" Space Dog said.
"If Beeper Moon doesn't stop
crying she'll drip herself away.
Then what will happen?

Space Dog did a quick loop
the loop . . .

. . . and got ready to land.

CHAPTER TWO

Planet Beep did not look at all
well.

Most of it was covered with
soft, wet, sticky green cheese.

The Beepers were huddled
together on the top of a hill.

Ma Beeper
was holding
an umbrella
and a bag FULL
of green-cheese
pies.

Grandpa
Beeper was
looking cross,
with his
boots on the
wrong feet.

Lily Beeper
was looking
worried.

Booty Beeper was peering
through a tube worm telescope
and Grandpa's spy glass.

"Hello," said Booty as Space
Dog landed beside him.
"You were AGES!"

"Sorry," said Space Dog.
"I was talking to Beeper Moon."

"THAT MOON!" said Grandpa.
He looked even crosser.

"It's ALL that
moon's fault!
Dripping
green cheese
all over us!

It's the end, if
you ask me.
That's what it
is. The end of
us Beepers.

We'll all be drowned in green cheese. You mark my words."
Lily Beeper began to snuffle.

Ma looked at Space Dog.
"Is it REALLY the end?"
Space Dog shook his head.
"WOOF! NO! We've just got to
stop Beeper Moon crying."

"CRYING?" exploded Grandpa.
"RUBBISH! That moon's
melting. Anyone can see that!!"

"She's very unhappy," said
Space Dog. "No one ever talks
to her."

"Of course they don't," Ma said.
"She shines at night, doesn't
she? And we Beepers need our
beauty sleep!"

"She doesn't start shining until EVER so late," said Grandpa. "Then there she is in the morning. RIDICULOUS!!!

No wonder she's melting away!"

"Hmm," said
Space Dog.
"Now – let me
think.

We need get
rid of all the
green cheese.

Then get
Beeper Moon
out in the sky
earlier – and
back to bed

BEFORE Big Sun comes up.
AND stop her crying!"

Grandpa snorted. "And how
are you going to do all that,
young dog?"

"Give him a chance, Grandpa,"
said Ma.

"That's right,"
said Space
Dog. "Now,
does anybody
know any
jokes?"

"JOKES???" Grandpa spluttered. "When we're drowning in green cheese? I never heard such RUBBISH!"

And he turned his back and sat down with a squelch.

"I know some really good
jokes," said Booty.

"No you don't," said Lily. "Your
jokes are AWFUL!"
"They're NOT!" said Booty.
"Space Dog, how do you stop a
tube worm smelling?"

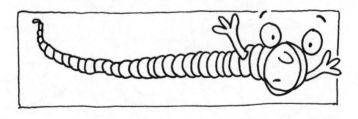

"I don't know," said Space Dog.
"How?"

"You hold its nose!" said Booty, and he cackled with laughter. Lily groaned loudly.

The tube worm shook its head and wriggled away.

"Hmm," said Space Dog.
"Booty – I think you are just
what Beeper Moon needs.
Can you fly?"

"ME? FLY?" said Booty.
"No – but I wish I could!"
"Silly young dog," muttered
Grandpa." As if we'd be sitting
here if we could fly."

"WOOF."
Space Dog
saw Ma's
umbrella.

"AHA! The very thing! Ma,
could we borrow that?"

"Of course,
dear," said Ma,
and she handed
him the big
stripy umbrella.

"Thank you," said Space Dog,
and he turned it upside down.
"Now – everyone hop in!"

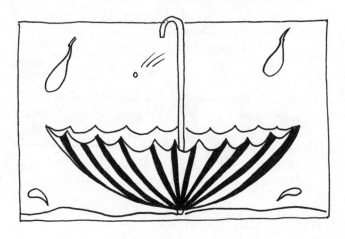

Ma, Grandpa
and Lily stared
at Space Dog.

Booty
grinned.

"WHAT?" said Ma and Grandpa.
"EEEEK!" said Lily.

Booty climbed in.
"Last one in is a sissy!" he
shouted.

And Lily tumbled after him.

"First of all," said Space Dog,
"we'll clean up Planet Beep.

Then we'll wake up Beeper
Moon. Oh – can I help you into
the umbrella, Ma Beeper?"
And Space Dog bowed as he
helped Ma climb in.

"I don't know what you're
planning," Grandpa
growled,
"but you'll
never get ME
in that thing! "

"WOOF!" said
Space Dog.
"Stay if you
want to – but
you may get
a little
giddy."

"I'm staying!" said Grandpa.

CHAPTER THREE

Ma, Lily and Booty sat in the
umbrella. Grandpa sat firmly on
top of his hill.Space Dog sighed.

"Here we go, then!" he said.
And up . . . and up . . . and up
they flew."

"WE'RE FLYING!" yelled Booty
and Lily. Ma was rather pale.
She held on tightly to the
umbrella handle.

Grandpa
stared after
them, his
mouth wide
open.

"Up . . . we . . . go!" puffed
Space Dog. At last they arrived
at Beeper Moon's bed cloud.

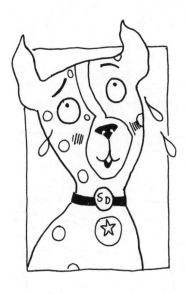

With one final
heave he
hooked the
umbrella onto
the edge. It
swung gently
to and fro.

"Oooooh!"
moaned Ma.
Lily held her
hand.

"Don't jump about too much,"
Space Dog said. "I'll be back in
no time!" He dived back down.

WEEEEEEEEEEEEEEEEEEE!!!!!
Space Dog began to fly round
and round Planet Beep.

"OI! STOP THAT, YOUNG
DOG!" Grandpa shouted.
"You're making us spin!"

But Space Dog didn't stop.
Round and round and round he
flew. Planet Beep began to turn
faster and faster and faster.

Grandpa went yellow. He clung
on tightly to the top of the hill.
Three large tube worms popped
out of the cheese. They wound
themselves round Grandpa.

WHEEEEEEEEEEEEEE!
Space Dog went faster still.

The planet spun and spun and spun . . . Soft sticky green cheese began to spin off in every direction. Drips and drops flew across the universe. Down on earth starspotters muttered to each other about strange green comets.

At last Space Dog slowed down.
Planet Beep rumbled to a stop.
Only a few
puddles and
pools of green
cheese shone
in the
sunlight.
It looked
much more
its usual self.

"It's all right, now, Grandpa!"
Space Dog said cheerfully.

Space Dog
waved, and
shot off to
collect the
umbrella.

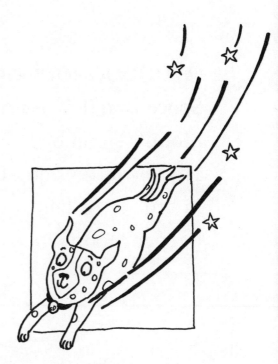

The umbrella was empty.

"WOOOOOOOOOOOOOOFF!
Space Dog flew round Beeper
Moon's cloud bed.
There was no sign of Ma . . . or
Booty . . . or Lily . . . or even of
Beeper Moon.

"WOWL!" howled Space Dog.
And he dived down below
Planet Beep to find them.

CHAPTER FOUR

If Space Dog had waited one
minute longer he would have
heard a strange noise.

HOO HOO! HOO HOO HOO!

 It was Beeper
Moon laughing.

Booty was
cackling . . .

. . . Lily was
giggling . . .

. . . and Ma
Beeper was
smiling.

"That's the best joke I've ever heard," Beeper Moon chortled. "Hold their noses! HOO! HOO!" Ma Beeper suddenly sat up.

"Did you hear that?" she asked. "I thought I heard Space Dog!"

"HOO! HOO!" Beeper Moon said. "Is that a joke?"

Ma shook her head. "Maybe we should get back in the umbrella."

"OH." Beeper Moon looked sad. "But we were having such fun."

"Can't you come out tonight?"
Booty asked. "If you come out
before eight we can tell more
jokes. But Lily and me, we have
to be in bed by then . . ."

Beeper Moon smiled.
"Oh, YES!" she said. "I'll come
out about half past five . . ."

"See you
then," said
Booty. He
scrambled
through the
cloud into
the umbrella.

Lily jumped after him.
Ma was just following when –
RRRRRRRRIPPPP!!!!

The cloud tore,
and Booty
and Lily
floated
further . . .
. . . and further
away . . .

"BOOOOOTY! LILY!" called Ma
as she clung to the edge of the
cloud.

"OH DEAR! OH DEAR!" said
Beeper Moon. She peered down
through the
cloud.

There was nothing any
of them could do.

Ma and Beeper
Moon watched
as Booty and
Lily floated on
down . . .

and down . . .

and down . . .

UNTIL . . .

WHOOOOOOOOOOOOSH!!!!!!
Space Dog came zooming up
from beneath.

Up and UP
they flew . . .
while Booty,
Lily, Ma and
Beeper Moon
cheered and
cheered.

On Planet Beep Grandpa waved
a tube worm until it was dizzy.

"Early bed
tonight," Ma
said as they
landed.
"But MA!" said
Booty. "Beeper
Moon's coming

out early just to hear my jokes!"
"Good," said Space Dog."There'll
be no more crying, then."

"That's all very well," said Grandpa.

"But if that moon NEVER cries, there'll be no more green-cheese pies!"

58

"Oooh!" said Ma. "I forgot!
My bag's full of them! Would
you like one, Space Dog?"

"No thank you," Space Dog
said. "I've got to be getting
back . . ." and he yawned.
"There'll be enough puddles of
cheese to keep you in pies for a
while yet, Grandpa."
"But what about when they
dry up?" Grandpa said. "Can
we call you?"

Space Dog yawned again.

"Of course you can," he said.

"That's what I'm here for.

To save the world."

He winked at Booty.

"And green-cheese

pies, too, of course!"

And off . . .

. . . and away

. . . he flew.